Tilly's Pony Tails

Moonshadow
the Derby winner

Tilly's Pony Tails
Moonshadow
the Derby winner

Pippa Funnell

Illustrated by Jennifer Miles

Orion
Children's Books

First published in Great Britain in 2010
by Orion Children's Books
New edition published 2012
by Orion Children's Books
a division of the Orion Publishing Group Ltd
Orion House
5 Upper St Martin's Lane
London WC2H 9EA
An Hachette UK Company

1 3 5 7 9 8 6 4 2

A catalogue record for this book is available from the British Library.

ISBN 978 1 4440 1434 1

www.orionbooks.co.uk
www.tillysponytails.co.uk

For my dear brother, Tim

Hello!

When I was little, I, like Tilly, was absolutely crazy about horses and ponies. All my books, pictures and toys had something to do with my four-legged friends.

I was lucky because a great friend of my mother's lent us a little woolly pony called Pepsi. He lived in the field at my best friend's house. I loved spending as much time as possible with him, but hated having to scrape all the mud off his shaggy winter coat. I used to lie in bed at night longing for the day I'd be able to have a smart horse all clipped and snuggled up in a stable with nice warm rugs.

My birthday treat every year was to go to The Horse of the Year Show, and

I remember going to Badminton and Burghley as a child. It was seeing top riders at these famous venues that gave me the inspiration to follow my dreams.

Now I've had the opportunity to ride some wonderful horses, all of whom have a special place in my heart. It's thanks to them that I have achieved my dreams and won so many competitions at the highest level. I still ride all day, every day, live, sleep and breathe horses and I love every minute of it.

Many of you will not be as used to horses as I am, so I have tried to include some of what I have learned in these books. At the back is a glossary so you can look up any unfamiliar words.

I hope you will enjoy reading the books in my series *Tilly's Pony Tails*, as much as I have enjoyed creating a girl who, like me, follows her passions. I hope that Tilly will inspire many readers to follow their dreams.

Love

One

It was a chilly winter morning. A layer of sparkly frost covered the yard at Silver Shoe Farm, but Tilly Redbrow didn't mind how cold it was. She was always happy to be up early, mucking out and feeding Magic Spirit.

Tilly knew how lucky she was to be helping at Silver Shoe.

Not every girl got the opportunity to spend so much time with her favourite horse, to ride every day, and have lessons with a teacher as good as Angela, Silver Shoe Farm's owner.

She carefully made her way across the icy ground towards Magic's stable. As she opened the door, he came to greet her. Tilly was glad to see his fleece-lined winter blanket hadn't come loose in the night. She was also grateful for her own Toggi gloves and woolly hat, which had been a Christmas present from her friends, Mia and Cally.

'Good morning, Magic. How are you today? It's freezing out there, but beautiful too – like a winter wonderland!'

Magic let out a snort, which looked like two puffs of smoke coming from his nostrils, visible in the cold air.

'Is that your impression of a dragon?'

He stared at her for a moment, then came close and nuzzled her shoulder. She stroked his neck, whispering softly and telling him how fantastic he was.

It wasn't long ago that Tilly had never
even been on a horse. She'd always loved
them. She'd read lots of pony magazines,
books and annuals. She'd watched hours
of Badminton and Burghley action on
television. Her bedroom walls were covered
with posters of ponies and horses. And
every night she would go to bed dreaming
about riding a horse of her own. She'd
hoped that one day it would happen, but
she'd never imagined it actually would.

Then, when she'd helped rescue Magic Spirit from a busy roadside, her life had changed completely.

Tilly refreshed Magic's bedding and gave him water and hay, then headed for the Silver Shoe club room. Her toes were frozen and she wanted to warm up with a mug of hot chocolate. The club room was a nice place to be at any time of year, but it was particularly welcoming in the winter. It was warm and cosy, with scruffy old sofas that you could sink into.

Mia was already in there, struggling to undo a purple padded gilet. Mia was one of Tilly's closest friends, along with Cally, and Becky, of course, her best friend from school. Cally was at Cavendish Hall, the same boarding school that Tilly's brother, Brook, also attended. Tilly, Mia and Cally had all shared a pony, Rosie, at one time,

before they'd grown too big for her. Now
Tilly rode Magic, and Cally had her dun
Connemara, Mr Fudge. Mia was still
looking, hoping she'd find her perfect horse
soon.

'I can't grip the zip. My fingers are
soooo cold!' said Mia.

'Let me help you,' said Tilly, as she
removed her gloves.

'I hope it's not this cold on Friday for
my birthday sleepover,' said Mia.

'We'll have to bring extra thick sleeping bags. I'm going to wear thermals and two big fleeces while I'm sleeping.'

'You won't be doing much sleeping,' said Mia, with a giggle. 'We'll be up all night telling spooky stories and having midnight feasts.'

'Not too spooky. It might be quite scary in the stables after dark.'

'The horses will look after us,' said Mia.

'True.'

The girls had been planning the sleepover for weeks. A group of them were going to stay overnight at Silver Shoe, as near to their favourite horses as they could be. Their parents hadn't been sure at first, but when Angela said that she and Duncan and some of the other stable hands would be up in the farm house and could keep an eye on them, everyone agreed. Tilly and Mia were very excited.

'Here, have this,' said Mia, passing Tilly a hot chocolate. 'Extra marshmallows.'

Just as the girls were getting comfy on

the sofas, the club room door swung open. It was Duncan, carrying a crate of canned drinks for the vending machine.

'Hi, girls. Frosty start, eh?'

He put the crate down on the worktop.

'Do you mind if I put the television on? I want to check the weather. If it's going to stay cold like this I'll need to get some extra grit down in the yard. I don't want anyone slipping.'

The television screen came to life. It was the local morning news. Uninterested, the girls turned back to each other and discussed party games for the sleepover.

'We should play the chocolate game, you know, where you have to eat a bar of chocolate with a knife and fork and wear gloves and a hat?'

'Or what about the one where everyone has to write the next line of a silly story?'

'Yeah. That's good. What else?'

Suddenly, an image on the screen caught Tilly's eye. It was a familiar one: a silvery grey horse galloping across a field.

Just like Magic Spirit! She blinked and looked closer.

'Who's that?' she said, mesmerised.

'That's Moonshadow,' said Duncan. 'Do you remember? He won the Derby last year. He's a fast one. Look at those long, limber legs. He looks extra special, like no ordinary horse.'

Duncan turned up the volume. The three of them watched and listened with interest.

'Local residents can see this famous racehorse, owned by the Archer's Engineering Racing Team, on the all-weather surface at Cosford County Winter Classic Flat Race this weekend. Good luck, Moonshadow. Good luck, Archer's Engineering. Let's hope he wins again…'

'Won't the ground be too hard for flat racing?' asked Tilly. 'It's so cold at the moment.'

'Good point,' said Duncan. 'Actually, it's only in recent years that flat racing has been able to take place all year round. It's thanks to special all-weather surfaces.'

'Cool,' said Mia. 'And Moonshadow's coming *here*!'

'Not here,' corrected Tilly. 'He's not actually coming to Silver Shoe.'

'No, I mean, he's coming to our area. He's probably going to stay in some really fancy stable somewhere.'

'You mean Silver Shoe isn't fancy?' said Duncan.

'No, I mean . . . I didn't . . . oh . . .'

17

'Don't worry,' said Duncan, laughing. 'You're right. A horse like Moonshadow is worth so much money. They'll put him in a top-end place, with all the latest kit. It'll have to be very high security though. There've been lots of problems with horse theft recently.'

'Really?' said Tilly. 'That's awful.'

'When there's big money involved, people get greedy.'

'I can't imagine what I'd do if someone stole Magic Spirit,' she said. She thought about it for a moment, then couldn't bear it. It was just too upsetting.

Two

Next morning before school, Tilly was in the long field, breaking up ice in the water trough. Lucky Chance was standing beside her, looking on curiously. Tilly had known Lucky since the day she was born. She'd even watched her birth. Now Lucky was an elegant little two-year-old whose training would soon begin.

'Everything fascinates you, doesn't it?' Tilly said.

Lucky dipped her nose into the trough

to inspect the lumps of ice.

'You'll be hard work to train, I bet. You'll be distracted every five minutes, constantly sticking your nose into everything. Never mind. That's what I like about you – you're a busy body!'

Tilly put down her shovel and gave Lucky a cuddle.

Suddenly, she was distracted by a glimpse of a large black horsebox bumping up the dirt road which ran along the back of the field. It was a road that was hardly ever used. It led to the back entrance of Silver Shoe, but it was overgrown with brambles.

'How odd! I wonder why it's driving up there?'

Lucky didn't seem bothered. She carried on prodding the ice with her nose.

'Must have taken a wrong turning,' Tilly said to herself.

She straightened Lucky's thick fleecy turn-out rug, which was green with blue trim and looked very stylish against her chestnut coat.

'There you go. Let's make sure you keep warm out here. See you later, Lucky.'

Tilly deliberately took the long route back to the yard, which joined with the dirt road. She wanted to find out where that horsebox had been going. Once she hit the track, she could see the squashed bramble bushes where it had squeezed through. Fortunately the muddy ground was frozen solid, so there wasn't too much mess.

Tilly followed the path right up to the back of the farm house and gardens. She sneaked through Angela's vegetable patch then headed towards the stables. She could see the shiny black horsebox in the distance. There was a man standing by the bumper, talking to Duncan and Jack Fisher, Angela's dad. He looked very serious.

What were they talking about? Tilly was intrigued. Not wanting to look as though she was spying, she decided to walk straight over, acting normal. She lifted her shoulders and marched forward.

'We really appreciate this,' she heard the man say. 'Particularly at such short notice. Obviously, you understand this is all in the strictest of confidence.'

'Of course,' said Duncan.

'Hi, Duncan. Hello, Jack,' said Tilly.

'Oh, hi, Tilly.'

There was an awkward moment of silence, then a snort and a foot stamp from inside the trailer. It was a sound Tilly knew well.

'Wait, that's not . . . Moonshadow, is it?' she exclaimed, spying the gold Archer's Engineering Racing Team logo on the man's jacket. She recognised it from the news feature they had watched the day before.

The man looked worried. There was another pause, then Duncan spoke.

'Don't worry, Mr Gibbens. This is Tilly Redbrow, one of our helpers. You can trust her.'

Tilly smiled and nodded and tried to look very trustworthy.

'I suppose it won't be possible to keep it entirely between ourselves,' said Mr Gibbens. 'People are sure to ask questions if he stays here for the whole weekend. It seems like a busy stable yard.'

Tilly's eyes widened.

'It's very busy, I'm afraid,' said Duncan.

'That's exactly what we wanted,' said Mr Gibbens. 'It's one of the reasons we selected Silver Shoe Farm. You're a solid, straightforward livery yard. It's the last place a pampered star like Moonshadow would be expected to hide.'

Duncan grinned. 'Gold-plated stables and diamond-encrusted water buckets?'

'Quite.'

'We won't be putting any extra security in place – we don't want to encourage suspicion.'

'That's fine,' said Jack Fisher.

'Does this mean,' said Tilly, with her hands on her hips, 'that Moonshadow, *the* Moonshadow, winner of the Derby, the one we saw on television, will be staying at Silver Shoe?'

'Um, yes.'

'But we're telling everyone that he's an average flat racer called Mr Chips, who's on a stop-over because his horsebox has broken down,' said Duncan, with a nod. 'You'll keep up the cover, won't you, Tilly?'

'Of course,' said Tilly, still slightly confused.

Moonshadow let out a little whinny.

'Please can I say hello?'

'Go on then,' said Mr Gibbens.

Tilly peered through the small door and made a soothing noise. Moonshadow gazed up at her with his bright eyes. He looked just like Magic, except his nose was darker, and though it was hard to tell from inside the trailer, he also seemed a bit taller. He was fully geared up with travel and tail bandages. He had a matching  black rug with the Archer's Engineering Racing Team logo embroidered in gold on the side.

'Wow!'

Tilly couldn't help but gasp. She was face-to-face with a true champion. Everything about him oozed power and sophistication. He let out a gentle snort and dipped his head.

'Hello, boy,' she said. 'Take a look at you!'

He stared back and she could sense him sizing her up, trying to decide whether he could trust her.

'Don't worry,' she said. 'I'm a friend. And while you're staying here at Silver Shoe, I'll look after you.'

Three

After school that day, Tilly couldn't wait
to tell Magic about their visitor. Although
it was supposed to be a secret, she knew
Magic wouldn't give it away to anyone!
She collected his saddle from the tack
room and went straight to his stable.

'Hey, gorgeous boy! Time for our riding
lesson with Angela.'

At the sight of the saddle, Magic
pricked his ears and quivered. Although
sometimes he could be cautious, he always

loved riding lessons with Tilly. She led him into the yard, tied him to a nearby post, then removed his winter rug and replaced it with his saddle. As she did this, she told him all about Moonshadow.

'He looks just like you. Slightly longer in the leg, I think. But you should see all the fancy stuff he's got. Everything is black with gold trim. He's like some sort of horse celebrity.'

Magic shook his mane and stared up at the sky. Tilly could tell he wasn't impressed by the black and gold trim.

'If – I mean – *when* you're a top celebrity horse, Magic, I'll make sure you get a nice set of matching tack too. Grey with silver trim? How would that be? To match your lovely coat.'

At this, Magic straightened and stood regally. He clearly liked the sound of his own gear. Tilly chuckled.

'Come on, Mr Fancy Pants. Let's go and see Angela.'

Angela was saying goodbye to her

previous students when Tilly and Magic arrived for their lesson. She waved and signalled for Tilly to get Magic warmed up. Tilly mounted and began circling the arena. She had done it a thousand times before, but Tilly always felt a tingle of thrill when she got up in the saddle. It felt so invigorating.

After five minutes of walking, they went into a trot and then a canter. She didn't want to ask Magic to work too hard too soon.

'Watch that left leg!' called Angela. 'You're gripping at the knee slightly.'

Trust Angela to spot the tiniest technical fault. Tilly didn't mind. That's what made Angela such a good rider, and a great teacher. Tilly knew if she paid attention to Angela's advice, especially the little things, her technique would keep improving.

She slowed down and tried to alter her position. As soon as she straightened herself up she found she was able to relax her upper leg. After a while the movement seemed to flow again and Tilly could tell Magic was relaxing too.

'Riders only grip with their thighs and knees to help them balance, so it's really important to work on your balance and sitting in the middle of the saddle, rather than slightly to left, or to the right,' explained Angela.

In the middle of the school Angela had a grid work exercise set up.

'Grid work is a great way to help you concentrate on your position over a fence,' she said. 'And it can really help the horse improve the shape of his jump. Now, Tilly, let's start with a trot pole on the floor before the little cross, and then I want you to come quietly out of trot, keeping very straight.'

Tilly repeated this twice, then Angela added a second bounce cross pole.

Tilly had never done a bounce, though she'd seen Angela do it once before. She knew it meant that Magic would have to immediately take off again after landing, without a stride in between. She trusted Magic, but that didn't stop her from feeling a bit nervous.

'Don't worry, Tilly,' said Angela, sensing her unease. 'Just let Magic work it out, but keep your lower leg very close and snuggled around him.'

Tilly tried to do what Angela said, but her nerves got the better of her. She tightened and pushed Magic too much at the trot pole, which made him speed up and do the exercise too quickly.

'Come again and just concentrate on a nice, relaxed approach,' said Angela. 'Bingo – excellent! Could you feel the difference there? Magic slowed his jump down then, which gave him time to use his body correctly.'

Tilly was pleased, and as Angela added more fences to the grid, she and Magic seemed to get better and better. When she finally came to a halt, Tilly was beaming.

'He was such a star!' she said excitedly, patting Magic's neck. 'You're not fazed by a challenge, are you, boy?'

Angela stared at Magic then looked up at Tilly.

'You know? I've just noticed. He looks so much like . . .'

She hesitated. Tilly could tell what she was thinking.

'Moonshadow?'

'Uh, yes.'

'I know he's here,' Tilly explained. 'Duncan told me. I saw him arriving this morning.'

'Well I'm sure people will work it out eventually. As long as the news doesn't get out of Silver Shoe.'

'Why do we have to be so secretive?'

'Unfortunately, Tilly, horse thieves often have plans for high profile champions like Moonshadow. He's a very valuable horse. Recently his owners have had to keep moving him from stable to stable in order to keep him safe. Luckily they won't find him at the stables he's supposed to be at this weekend, but if rumour gets out that he's here . . .'

'Poor Moonshadow.'

'You'll help us keep it quiet, won't you?'

'Of course.'

Suddenly Tilly saw a flash of purple gilet. It was Mia, leading Aladdin, one of the riding school horses, towards the arena. Tilly thought for a moment.

'Can I at least tell Mia?' she asked. 'She'll be cross if I know a secret that she doesn't.'

Angela smiled.

'I guess we can make an exception there.'

Four

'He's beautiful,' said Mia, as she peered over the door into Moonshadow's stable. 'Hello there,' she called softly.

She reached out her hand and tried to coax Moonshadow towards her. He looked at her for a moment, then backed away further into the shadows. Mia made a clicking noise with her tongue, but still Moonshadow didn't come to her.

'He's very shy,' she said, disappointed.

'Maybe he's wary of strangers,' said Tilly.

'Or bored? If he's always being moved around, he probably never gets the chance to feel settled.'

'Like when my dad goes abroad with his work,' said Mia. 'And everyone says, 'Ooh, how exciting and glamorous!' But Dad doesn't think so. He says it's dreary and lonely.'

Tilly stared at Moonshadow. Whether he was bored and lonely or not, he was definitely in good physical condition. He looked fit and ready to run. The shine of his coat highlighted his good health. Tilly imagined how wonderful he'd look when he was racing, remembering the footage she'd seen of him on the television.

'Do you think he'll be able to make an appearance at my sleepover?' said Mia. 'As a guest of honour.'

'I doubt it,' said Tilly. 'We're meant to keep his identity secret, remember?'

'Talking of parties, we need to blow up the balloons and decorate the barn. We can't leave it all until Friday. I want streamers and banners and gold confetti and matching plates and cups and napkins. My mum's bought us loads of food. Come on, let's go to the club room and start getting things ready.'

'Um, in a little while,' said Tilly, hesitating. 'I want to spend some more time with Moonshadow. He won't be here for long.'

'Suit yourself,' said Mia. 'But don't be ages.'

Then she swivelled on the heels of her jodhpur boots and walked away. Tilly smiled. She knew Mia didn't mean to be impatient – she was just worried about getting everything done for her party.

'Give me a minute, then I'll join you,' she called after her.

When Tilly was alone with Moonshadow, she leaned over the door and beckoned to him. As she did this, her horsehair bracelets – the one she'd had since she was a baby, given to her by her birth mum before she died, and the other she'd made from Magic Spirit's tail-hairs, slipped down from her sleeve and caught Moonshadow's attention.

'Come on then, boy,' she whispered. 'Come and have a look.'

His ears pricked up and his gaze fixed

on Tilly. It was the same look he'd given her when she'd seen him in the horsebox earlier, as though he was wondering what to make of her. She turned slightly to the side and stood very still, so as not to appear threatening. Then she made a low, quiet humming sound.

Slowly, Moonshadow stepped towards her.

'Oh, you are beautiful,' she whispered, as he came into view.

When he was close enough, Tilly reached out her hand and invited him to explore it. Like all the other horses she knew, Moonshadow was immediately interested in the bracelets. He nibbled and sniffed them, then bobbed his nose towards her face. The whiskers of his muzzle tickled. Tilly giggled.

'Nice to meet you,' she said. 'So you *are* a friendly horse after all.'

She ran her hands along Moonshadow's neck and shoulder. His coat felt as silky as it looked.

'You must have a good diet to get a coat this gorgeous. And lots of careful grooming. Oh, I'd love to . . .'

Suddenly, Tilly was overwhelmed by the urge to brush Moonshadow's coat.

'I know I'm probably not supposed to,' she said quietly. 'But, well, this might be my only opportunity – my one chance to get close to a horse as famous as you, a Derby winner! You won't mind, will you?'

Moonshadow looked at her, then seemed to nod towards his grooming kit, which was in a black lacquered box just outside the stable. This might have been a coincidence, but Tilly liked to think it was an invitation.

She crouched in front of the box. There was a black sticker on the front, hiding the gold logo she'd seen on the horsebox and blankets. She lifted the lid. Everything inside was immaculate, brand new and top quality. Except for one particular body brush. Instinctively, Tilly picked it up and looked at it closely.

It was old and well-used. But she knew.

'I guess this is your favourite,' she said, holding the brush out to Moonshadow.

He turned slightly, as though presenting himself for grooming. Tilly folded his rug back and ran the brush along the length of his body. It glided effortlessly, rippling along the curves of his muscular frame. Seeming soothed by the sensation, he lowered his head.

'Does that feel nice?' she asked, as she swept the brush over his hindquarters.

When she reached his tail, which was the same silvery-grey as his coat, she combed her fingers through it and collected the stray hairs.

'I'm sure these will come in useful somehow,' she whispered.

Five

After school on Friday, Tilly didn't go straight to Silver Shoe as she usually did, but went home to pack for her overnight stay at the stables. Her mum helped her get together all the things she needed. They sat on Tilly's bed and made a pile of warm clothes.

'Make sure you've got a thick pair of socks,' said Tilly's mum. 'Really, I don't know why you girls are so keen to sleep out in the stables during winter weather like this.'

'For fun,' said Tilly. 'We don't mind a bit of cold. And this way, we get to have our horses around too.'

Tilly's mum rolled her eyes and smiled.

'Well, here you are then,' she said. 'This is your dad's extra warm sleeping bag. It should keep you nice and snug. And here's your pony pillow cover.'

Tilly grabbed the cover and hugged it close – it was a favourite from when she was younger. It had been through the wash so many times that it was faded and bobbled, which made it even more comforting. She sighed and breathed in its familiar smell.

'I didn't know you'd kept this!' she said.

'Mums keep all sorts of things,' replied her mum, smiling. 'Because before we know it, our children are all grown up.'

She brushed her hand down the back of Tilly's head. Tilly turned and gave her a quick hug.

'You're the best mum ever!' she said.

Even though she was adopted, the
Redbrows were Tilly's family through and
through. She wanted her mum to know
how much she loved her. It didn't make a
difference that she and Brook, her newly-
discovered brother, were trying to find out
about their birth mum. Tilly knew there
was room in her life for two mums.

Just then, her mobile beeped.

'It's Brook,' she said. 'Must be sibling sixth sense! I was just thinking about him, and now he texts.'

HEY T. CHECK YOUR EMAILS.

WE'VE HAD A MESSAGE FROM CHIEF FOUR PAWS! X

Tilly gasped. Chief Four Paws was the head of the Native American tribe that Tilly and Brook had been researching. They'd been told about similarities between their own horsehair bracelets and the bracelets worn by the tribe members. They'd also seen photographs of their mum, wearing Native American clothes and standing next to a black horse, a Mustang. When they'd got in touch with the tribe to find out if their mum had ever visited, Chief Four Paws had replied and said one of the tribal elders was sure he remembered her.

'Exciting!' said Tilly's mum. 'Go and check.'

Tilly rushed downstairs to the living

room and, after some negotiation (involving the promise of left-over midnight feast sweets), managed to get Adam to end his game of Zombie Crusher IV. She logged on to her emails and checked her inbox. Sure enough, there was a message from Chief Four Paws, entitled, 'Horsehair Charm Bracelets'.

Dear Brook and Tilly,

I hope you're both well. I hear it's very cold in England at the moment. Britain is known for its snowy winters, isn't it? The nights get very cold here, but we have not seen any snow yet.

Anyway, I'm attaching some photos of our tribe members wearing their horsehair bracelets. As you can see, they're just like yours. We wear them as charms, one for each horse we ride. We believe they help us to understand our animals and keep them safe. It's a tradition that goes back centuries, from when our ancestors were watching over free-roaming Mustangs and protecting them from horse rustlers.

I'm fascinated to hear more about your story. It's intriguing to think that a little bit of our tribe's history has made it all the way to England.

Kind regards,
Chief Four Paws

Tilly opened the photo attachments and studied the images. The bracelets were exactly the same as the ones she and Brook wore – one fine plait of horsehair, connected with a little metal clasp. One of the photos showed a male tribe member who was wearing several

bracelets forming a thick band around his wrist. He must be wonderful with horses to have so many bracelets, she thought.

Tilly stared at the image, studying the man's eyes. They were dark and friendly, with laughter creases at the corners. Something about them reminded her of Brook. She ran her finger over the plaits of her own bracelets, and with her heart beating fast, replied to Brook's text.

HOW AMAZING! JUST LIKE OURS! DID YOU SEE THE ONE OF THE MAN WHO WEARS LOTS OF THEM? IT FEELS LIKE WE'RE STARTING TO MAKE SENSE OF EVERYTHING. SPEAK SOON. X

Tilly's mum appeared over her shoulder.

'Ooh. Photos. You'll have to send Chief Four Paws some pictures of you and Magic, won't you? We'd better leave soon, Tilly. You don't want to be late for this sleepover. Oh, I thought you might need this . . .'

She handed Tilly a large, high-powered torch.

'Mum! We're only sleeping at Silver Shoe. It's not like we're trekking into deep, dark jungle or anything!'

'Well, you never know.'

Six

When Tilly arrived at the farm, Mia was already there, opening the door of the big barn, which was where they were going to spend the night. She saw Tilly at the five-bar gate and waved.

'Come and help me. I'm doing the finishing touches to the decorations. It's too exciting.'

Tilly nodded, but before she ran over to Mia, she couldn't help pausing to check on Moonshadow. She peeped over the door of his stable, and saw him relaxing inside, keeping himself to himself. His stable was two doors down from Magic's. Tilly wondered if they'd met each other yet and noticed how alike they were.

'Hurry up, Tilly!' Mia's voice echoed round the yard. 'We've got a party to prepare!'

'I'm coming.'

As Tilly turned, she saw Magic's head bobbing over the stable door. He'd obviously heard her voice and wanted to see where she was. Tilly knew she couldn't say hello to Moonshadow and not to Magic.

'Hello, handsome boy!'

He nuzzled her ear then glanced over at Moonshadow's stable.

'Don't feel jealous, Magic. He's just a visitor – a celebrity visitor – but, really, you've got nothing to worry about. You're every bit as gorgeous as him – and more! I'll be staying at Silver Shoe tonight. Will you like that? Mia will be here. And Cynthia. And Cally. She's coming over with

Mr Fudge. In fact, here they are now.'

Mr Fudge gave a little whinny as Cally led him into the yard. Tilly waved.

'Hi, Mr Fudge. Hi, Cal. Nice top.'

Cally was wearing a new dusky pink fleece, which looked good with her cream jodhpurs.

'Thanks. Hey, two Magics! How did that happen?'

Moonshadow had appeared at the stable door. Cally was staring between him and Magic with a look of confusion.

'Ah,' said Tilly. She was desperate to tell Cally about Silver Shoe Farm's special guest, but she knew she shouldn't.

Just in time, Mia marched over holding a bag of cushions.

'Right, you two! Stop dawdling and get busy with this lot. Let's make it as comfy and warm as possible in that barn.'

Half an hour later, the big barn looked fit for a fabulous party. The girls had made a table from one of the hay bales and laid out all the party food. There were crisps, sausage rolls, cheese-on-sticks, pizza, fairy cakes, and plenty of Silver Shoe homemade lemonade. They'd made a little den from the rest of the hay bales and covered the ground with blankets and cushions.

They'd even brought party food for the horses. There was a bag of apples and carrots, and a packet of mints as a special treat. It was exciting to think they'd all be spending the night at Silver Shoe.

At about six-thirty, the sleepover officially began. Cally poured the lemonade. Cynthia got the music going on her MP3 player. Mia unwrapped her presents – a sparkly bridle from Cynthia, who adored anything glittery, and a book about show jumping from Cally.

'Happy birthday,' said Tilly, as she handed Mia her present – a pair of padded riding gloves covered in horseshoe

 wrapping paper. 'To keep your fingers warm. I hope they fit.'

'Thanks,' said Mia, as she tried them on. 'They're perfect!'

Then she sighed, and Tilly thought she looked a little upset.

'What? Don't you like them?'

'No, I love them. I was just . . . I was kind of hoping you'd give me one of your horsehair bracelets, that's all.'

'Oh,' said Tilly, feeling bad.

Although Mia was one of her closest friends, it was true she was one of the only ones Tilly hadn't yet made a bracelet for. It wasn't deliberate. The right horse and the right time hadn't come up. Tilly's horsehair bracelets were precious. They couldn't just be given away without good reason.

'Don't worry. I'll make you one when the time is right,' said Tilly, giving Mia a hug. 'It'll be extra special.'

Mia smiled, reassured. 'Okay. Let's think up some creepy ghost stories to tell at midnight!'

'Do we have to?' said Cynthia.

'I like the one about the haunted farm house,' whispered Tilly.

'And the headless horseman,' added Cally.

Suddenly, they heard a loud snort from next door. The girls jumped and screamed, then fell about laughing.

'Please don't spook me out,' said Cynthia. 'I won't be able to sleep.'

'What makes you think we'll be doing any sleeping?' said Mia. 'I've got stacks of games for us to play.'

Mia was interrupted by the sound of whinnying.

'That sounds like Magic,' said Tilly. 'He knows I'm here. He's probably wondering why I'm not coming to see him.'

At eight-fifteen, Magic was still restless. Duncan and Angela came down from the farm house to say good night, bringing flasks of steaming hot chocolate with them.

'Remember, if it gets too cold for you out here, you can always come up to the house,' said Angela.

'I don't know about too cold,' said Tilly. 'I've got the warmest sleeping bag in the world. But it might be a noisy night.'

'Magic's being a party pooper,' said Cynthia.

'He's not a party pooper,' said Cally. 'He just wants to see Tilly.'

'I've tried to reassure him,' said Tilly, 'but he keeps calling me. Perhaps I should try again.'

'I'll come with you,' said Duncan. 'Grab a torch. It's dark out there.'

Seven

As soon as Magic saw Tilly and Duncan, he went quiet. Tilly stroked his nose.

'You silly sausage,' she said. 'I'm not far away. You've got nothing to worry about.'

Once he was settled and Angela and Duncan had returned to the house, Tilly went back to her friends and got into her sleeping bag. They shared out bags of sweets.

'So, who's got any gossip?' asked Cally.

'Don't you think Angela and Duncan are madly in love with each other?' said Mia.

'Are they going out?' asked Cynthia.

'No one knows for sure,' said Cally. 'They spend lots of time together and clearly they're made for each other. If they're not officially boyfriend and girlfriend by the summer, I think we should force them!'

They talked for ages about how they could set up Angela and Duncan, and completely lost track of time.

'I've got some other news,' said Tilly eventually, looking down at her horsehair bracelets. 'Brook and I had an email from the Native American tribe, from Chief Four Paws. He sent us photos of members of his tribe wearing horsehair bracelets. They're just like ours.'

'Cool,' said Cally, as she stifled a yawn.

'Does that mean you're descended from the tribe?' asked Cynthia.

'Well, it's possible. It feels kind of

weird, in a good way. And it makes sense, given that Brook and I like horses so much.'

'Love them, more like,' corrected Mia.

Cally let out another yawn. Then so did Cynthia.

'What time is it?'

'Ooh. It's gone ten.'

'Come on,' said Mia. 'I want to stay up till past midnight. Let's play a game. Wink Murder or something?'

But as she said this, she started snuggling into her sleeping bag, and before she knew it she was curled on her side, drifting off to sleep.

'So much for staying up all night,' muttered Tilly.

No one responded. She glanced around and realised Cally and Cynthia were also asleep.

Tilly didn't feel tired. There was too much on her mind. She was half-listening out for Magic to make sure he was okay, but most of all, she was thinking about

Chief Four Paws and her birth mum and beautiful wild Mustangs.

A while later, a loud neigh echoed around the yard. Tilly stared up at the dark ceiling. Was she dreaming? Had she finally fallen asleep?

She wasn't sure. Then she heard it again.

A long strained cry.

It wasn't a happy sound. She sat up. Everything was quiet. Maybe it was a horse having a bad dream, or calling out in their sleep. Instinctively Tilly wanted to check on Magic and the other horses.

She got to her feet and crouched over Mia, shaking her gently.

'Mia! Mia? Wake up!'

Mia stirred.

'Huh?'

'It's me. I'm sorry, Mia. I didn't want to wake you, but I heard something. I need to check the horses. Will you come with me?'

Mia turned over and shut her eyes again.

'Uh, go back to sleep, it's probably nothing.'

Tilly looked at the barn door, which opened out to the cold, dark yard. She didn't like the idea of going alone.

'Please?' she said.

'Oh, all right, all right! Just give me a minute!'

The girls stood up and zipped their fleeces. They took the torch Tilly's mum had given her and opened the barn door.

Outside, the air was still. The moonlight gave everything a silvery shimmer and now the only sound was a distant owl hoot.

'What did you hear?' asked Mia.

'A neigh.'

'A neigh? Like, duh, this is a livery yard! Of course we're going to hear a few neighs and whinnies. Doesn't mean we have to get out of bed and stand in the freezing cold.'

Tilly shrugged.

'I don't know. All I can say is that it sounded kind of odd. Maybe I imagined it.'

'Great. So we got out of our nice warm sleeping bags, all because you imagined you heard a neigh . . . in a livery yard!'

Before Mia had a chance to finish, the neigh in question came again, followed by the sound of human voices.

Tilly and Mia both froze.

'Where did it come from?' whispered Tilly, glancing round the stable blocks.

'And who are they?' gasped Mia, pointing towards the disused dirt road that led away from the farm house gardens. In the distance, a group of men were trying to coax a grey horse into the back of an old van. They'd covered its face with a blanket, presumably to disorientate it.

The horse was resisting fiercely, stamping its feet and trying to pull away.

Tilly's heart began to race.

'Horse thieves,' she croaked, barely able to get her words out. 'They're taking Moonshadow!'

'Don't let them see us,' whimpered Mia.

The girls pressed themselves closely to the wall of the big barn. Tilly hid the torch. Her legs were wobbly with nerves. She could feel Mia trembling beside her.

'What do we do?'

'We need to get to the farm house,' said Tilly. 'We need to tell Duncan and Angela.'

They heard another neigh. This time, the sound of it made Tilly feel breathless and faint.

'Something's not right,' she said.

'Of course it's not,' said Mia. 'They're stealing Moonshadow!'

'No. Something else. It's . . .'

Then she gasped as the horrible reality dawned on her.

It wasn't Moonshadow being herded into that van. His stable door was still shut tight.

It wasn't Moonshadow. It was Magic!

Eight

Tilly ran to Magic's stable. The door was unbolted and swinging slightly. The sight of the empty space inside was wrenching.

'We've got to do something!' she said, her eyes brimming with tears. 'They can't take him!'

It felt as though her heart was being torn into pieces. Momentarily, she had the urge to run after Magic, to stop the thieves from pushing him into the van, but Mia pulled her back.

'Wait. We've got to be careful, Tilly. Those guys could be dangerous. We don't know.'

Sensing her friend's distress, Mia took hold of Tilly's hands. Somehow, she was managing to stay calm. She helped Tilly get control.

'Listen to me. It's going to be okay. We won't let them take Magic. No way. But we've got to be sensible. We need a plan.'

Tilly took a deep, shuddering breath.

'That's better,' said Mia, as she rubbed

Tilly's shoulders. 'Now. What we need is time. Magic will only be able to resist those men for so long, and once he's in the van . . .'

She shook her head.

'Anyway, let's not think about that. We'll get him back. You go straight to the farm house, Tilly. Raise the alarm with Duncan and Angela. Get them to call the police. I'll create a diversion.'

'What will you do?'

'Uh, don't worry, I'll think of something.'

Tilly paused.

'Why not let Moonshadow out of his stable?' she suggested. 'If the thieves see another grey horse and realise they might have the wrong one, they might panic. It's risky. Oh, maybe it's a bad idea . . .'

'It's genius!' said Mia.

The girls high-fived then ran off in separate directions.

Mia approached Moonshadow carefully. She worried he wouldn't co-operate. He'd always seemed so shy before.

'Please,' she whispered, holding her hand out to him. 'You have to come with me, boy. No time to waste. One of our horses is in danger.'

Despite the pressure, she remained calm and kept her voice as low and soft as possible. Moonshadow pricked his ears and took a step towards her.

By the time Tilly reached the farm house, Mia was leading Moonshadow from his stable. She watched as they walked directly towards the men. The sight of it made her heart race.

'Please be safe,' she sighed, tugging her horsehair bracelets. 'Please!'

Then she knocked on the door, rang the bell and called out – anything to get someone's attention.

Moments later, a sleepy-eyed Duncan was standing in front of her.

'Hey, Tilly,' he croaked. 'So it finally

got too cold for you? Come on in.'

Tilly shook her head.

'It's an emergency! Thieves have got Magic! They're trying to take him in a van!'

She talked so quickly, the words stumbled out.

'Is this a joke?' said Duncan. Then he saw the look in Tilly's eyes.

He grabbed his mobile, which was by the door, and dialled.

'Go inside,' he said. 'Go and get Angela. Quickly. She's in her room.'

Tilly woke Angela and explained what was happening.

'What about the other girls? We've got to get them up to the house,' said Angela, as she tugged on a pair of boots. 'We can't leave them in the barn. It could be dangerous.'

Tilly didn't dare explain what Mia was up to. She thought of her, out there with the thieves, with Moonshadow, with Magic. It was all happening so quickly it was hard to think straight.

'Let's go and get them,' said Angela. 'Stay with me.'

Just as they got to the bottom of the stairs, a chorus of neighs filled the air, followed by loud shouting.

'What's happening?' said Tilly, peering through the front door.

Moonshadow and Magic were in the yard, bucking and shaking their heads. It looked as though the plan had worked. The two horses were together. They were clearly distressed, but they were free!

Duncan was standing against the wall
of the big barn. He was still on the phone.
The shouting was coming from the thieves,
who were, by the sound of it, stuck on the
dirt road trying to get their van started.

Angela's hand was on Tilly's shoulder, holding her steady, but Tilly couldn't wait. She lurched forward and ran straight to Magic. As soon as he saw her, he stopped fretting and calmed.

'I thought they'd taken you,' she sobbed, relief flooding over her. 'I thought you'd gone!'

Magic dropped his head to her shoulder, shut his eyes and stood very still, as if relishing every moment of their togetherness. Tilly hugged him and felt like she never wanted to let go.

'I love you so much,' she said, and for a moment, nothing else in the world existed but her and Magic.

After a while, Tilly was vaguely aware of the activity going on around her: of a sleepy Cally and Cynthia emerging from the big barn and asking what was going on; of Angela telling them not to worry and leading them to the house; of Duncan and a couple of the other live-in stable hands running towards the dirt road to see if they could hold the horse thieves; of a distant siren and the flashing blue lights of a police van; of Mia.

Mia! What about Mia?

With the shock of everything, Tilly realised she didn't know where Mia was. Anxiously, she looked around. There was no sign of her. Then she spotted Moonshadow at the far end of the yard, standing next to the five-bar gate, the moonlight bouncing off his glossy, silver coat. Mia was standing with him. She'd managed to calm him, and was holding tight to his halter, stroking his neck soothingly.

'Mia!' Tilly called, then ran over and hugged her friend.

'Tilly! Is Magic okay?'

'I think he's fine. I'm just so glad he's safe. Are you okay?'

Mia looked up at Moonshadow. She patted his nose and rubbed his cheek.

'We're good. To be honest, it's all a bit of a blur.'

'You've been so brave,' said Tilly. 'You saved Magic and Moonshadow!'

'It was your idea,' said Mia.

'But you did it. When I knew they'd taken Magic, I just crumbled. You were the one who kept it together!'

'I guess I did, didn't I?'

Mia smiled and straightened her shoulders. Her cheeks glowed.

'What a sleepover!'

Nine

Tilly woke the next morning in her own bed. It took a while for her to remember everything that had happened. She stared at the ceiling and ran it through in her mind.

She remembered her parents had come to collect her. She'd been worried they'd be cross about having to get up at two in the morning, but they were fine. They'd just been relieved that she and Magic were safe. She remembered the feeling of climbing between her warm, clean bed sheets, and how comforting they'd felt. And she remembered her last thoughts before she fell asleep, hoping Magic was as warm and comfortable in his stable.

'Tilly?'

Her mum knocked softly on the bedroom door. Tilly peered at her alarm clock. It was nine-thirty. For the first time in months, she'd slept in.

'Magic!' she exclaimed, sitting up. 'Who's going to feed Magic?'

'Don't worry,' said Tilly's mum, coming in with a tray of breakfast. 'It's all sorted. Angela and the others are looking after the horses this morning. We figured you girls could do with a lie-in after such an eventful night.'

Tilly smiled at her mum, then she pushed her long dark hair to one side and took the breakfast tray. Although she loved getting up early to groom and feed the horses at Silver Shoe, she was secretly glad to have the morning off.

Tilly's mum kissed her forehead and sat on the end of the bed.

'You had us worried,' she sighed. 'You and that horse!'

'What will happen to the thieves?'

'They're in police custody at the moment. Hopefully they'll be charged and that will be that. I heard one of the police officers saying they've been trying to catch them for months. They're a well-known gang.'

Suddenly, Tilly's little brother, Adam, appeared in the doorway.

'Tell me everything! Tell me everything! Were they really scary?' he said, hopping across the floor and up on to the bed. 'Were they baddies? Did they have guns? Were they wearing masks?'

Tilly guessed she'd gone up in her brother's Cool-o-Meter.

'Hi, Adam,' she said.

'Mum says you and Mia were really brave. I used to think Mia was a bossy-boots, but you can tell her from me, I've changed my mind. Now I think she's actually quite cool.'

Tilly and her mum laughed. Tilly reached for her phone and sent a text to Mia:

HI, HERO-MIA. JST 2 LET U KNOW, ADAM NOW THINKS UR
QUITE COOL! ME 2. C U LATER? X

Seconds later, a reply came:

NICE LIE-IN! TELL ADAM, I'M TOUCHED.
GOING 2 SS AT 10:30. X

'Can you drive me over to the farm this morning?'

'But Magic's all taken care of. You must be shattered,' said Tilly's mum. 'Don't you want a day off?'

Tilly shrugged and pulled a face.

'I guess it was silly of me to even think that you would,' said her mum, smiling. 'I'll take you on the way to Adam's football.'

When Tilly arrived at Silver Shoe, Mia was already there. So, too, were Moonshadow's trainers and owners, including Mr Gibbens. Tilly recognised them immediately from the sleek black and gold horsebox. They were all standing in the yard, talking to Angela, Duncan and Jack Fisher.

'Ah, here she is,' said Duncan. 'Our other little super-sleuth! This is Tilly Redbrow.'

Tilly slid up next to Mia, who was beaming from ear-to-ear.

'Hello again,' said Mr Gibbens. 'You told Moonshadow you'd look after him – we're just glad you were true to your word. Thank you so much.'

'It was nothing,' said Tilly, blushing.

'As a thank you,' said Mia, gripping Tilly's arm, 'we've been invited to watch Moonshadow's race tomorrow. From the Archer's Engineering luxury box! How cool is that?!'

Tilly's eyes widened.

'You can bring your family and friends too,' explained Mr Gibbens. 'We'll lay everything on for you – food, drink, the lot. It's our treat!'

'Just remember your best hats,' said the woman with him.

Tilly looked at Mia. Now she knew why she was smiling so much. A day at the races, no expense spared. Her stomach somersaulted with excitement.

'Can invite my brother, Brook? And Becky? And Cally? And Cynthia? And . . .?'

'You can invite whoever you want. It's the biggest, most luxurious box at the course. Usually it's hired by wealthy businessmen, but we've insisted they reserve it exclusively for you. You'll be treated like royalty.'

'And we're sorry your horse, Magic Spirit, had to go through all that trauma,' said another man, whose black and gold jacket said 'Horse Trainer'. 'It must have been very frightening for him – and for you. We hope he's okay. If there's anything we can do to help, just let us know.'

But in her heart Tilly knew the one thing that would help Magic to recover from the experience was her love and attention.

'The good news is,' said Mr Gibbens, 'those thieves will go to jail, and that will keep lots of other horses safe for years to come.'

'Hear, hear!' said Duncan.

Everyone nodded. From the stables behind them came a loud neigh. It sounded like one of the horses was agreeing with Duncan, but Tilly knew otherwise. It was Magic.

'Er, I'd better go and check on Magic,' she said. 'I guess I'll see you at the races tomorrow. Thank you.'

'Thank *you*,' said Mr Gibbens.

Magic was waiting for Tilly in his stable.

'Hey, boy. Were you calling me?'

Immediately, he came towards her.
She felt the nervous pulse of his blood, the
tension in his body. He was still agitated by
the night's adventures.

'It's okay. I'm here now,' she said
reassuringly. 'You're safe. I'll never let
anything like that happen to you again.'

She held his face close to hers and let
him feel the warmth of her skin against his.

'Nothing will come between us, I
promise,' she whispered.

And as she said these words, and
stroked his nose, gradually his anxiety
disappeared.

Ten

'Well, this is a treat!' said Mrs Redbrow, as they stepped inside the Archer's Engineering sponsored box. A waiter wearing a black shirt gave her a glass of champagne.

Everyone had been thrilled when Tilly and Mia invited them. Brook cancelled a riding lesson so he could make it. Becky postponed a shopping trip. Tilly's mum rushed out to buy hats for her and Tilly. Tilly's was neat and small with a small cluster of red feathers on the side. It went perfectly with her cherry red prom dress. And although, in general, she hated wearing anything other than riding gear, today she felt special.

'You look great,' said Mia.

'You too,' said Tilly.

It was amazing to think this was all happening because of them.

'It's so glam,' said Mia. 'Look at everything.'

The box was decorated with black lacquered furniture and gold ribbons. At the back, there was a table overflowing with delicious finger food – prawns, salmon, and miniature sandwiches. In the middle there was a huge chocolate fountain, which Tilly's brother, Adam, couldn't take his eyes off.

The front of the box was entirely glass, and looked down, with the best view, over the racecourse. Tilly and Mia stood in front of it. Below them, hundreds of people were milling around, waiting for the main race to

begin. They were wearing thick overcoats
and jiggling about to keep warm.

'Not like us, eh?' said Mia, scoffing.

'This is great,' said Brook, coming to
join them. 'Thanks for inviting me. I've
always wanted to know what it's like to
watch a race from one of these boxes.'

'You scrub up all right,' said Mia cheekily, admiring his smart trousers and shirt.

'Of course he does,' said Tilly. 'He's my brother!'

The three of them pressed up against the glass to watch the proceedings.

'Looks like things are about to get going,' said Tilly. 'They're moving the horses into the starting stalls.'

'Which one's our boy?' said Brook.

'There he is,' said Mia. 'The grey at the far end, with his black and gold colours.'

'Are you sure that's not Magic?' said Brook. 'They're so alike!'

'Quite sure,' said Tilly, with a wry smile.

An announcement came over the tannoy introducing the race. Everyone gathered round to look at the starting gates. They could see everything so clearly, it was better than watching it on television.

Tilly had her fingers crossed. She couldn't quite believe it, but Moonshadow was her lucky number seven. It had to be a good omen. She just knew it.

'Go, Moonshadow!' called Mia's dad, waving his betting slip. 'This is the one!'

'You can do it!' said Tilly's dad. He didn't normally make bets, but on this occasion, encouraged by Mia's dad, he'd decided to take a chance.

Silence filled the room. Tilly bit her lip nervously and glanced over at Duncan. This was just as exciting as when they'd watched Red Admiral win at the Cosford race meeting, with Duncan riding. She wondered if he was picturing himself out there now, wearing Moonshadow's colours, steeling himself for the ride of his life.

The starting gun fired and the gates sprang open. They were off!

Moonshadow was behind at first, for the first furlong, but then, as if from nowhere, his legs began to power up. His strong strides ploughed up the field, and it wasn't long before he was the lead horse. By the middle of the fifth furlong no one could get close to him.

'That's what I call a Derby winner!' said Duncan, impressed.

Tilly could only nod in agreement. She was dumbstruck by Moonshadow's power and grace.

As he crossed the finish line, everyone cheered with delight.

'I'm rich! I'm rich!' said Tilly's dad.

'Not with a one pound bet, you're not,' said her mum. Everyone laughed.

Mia grabbed Tilly by the waist and gave her a huge hug.

'Oh, I nearly forgot,' said Tilly, and she reached into the little red bag that matched her dress. 'You know what I said about finding the right horse to make a bracelet from, especially for you?'

Mia looked at her.

'Well, I've found him, haven't I? Here you go.'

She pulled out a delicate silver-grey plait of tail-hair and fastened it around Mia's wrist.

'It's Moonshadow's. It'll remind you of the time you were so brave and helped save him and Magic Spirit. It's my way of saying thank you.'

'Thank you so much, Tilly!' said Mia. 'This is the best present ever!'

'And it's a pretty precious bracelet,' said Brook. 'The tail-hairs of a famous Derby winner! You don't see that every day.'

'All Tilly's bracelets are precious,' said Cally.

'Thanks, guys,' said Tilly, smiling at her friends.

She opened her arms for a group hug.

'I'm so happy! This is the best reward!' said Mia.

Tilly smiled and closed her eyes. She was happy too, but to her, the best reward of all was just knowing that Magic was safe and sound.

Pippa's Top Tips

In the winter, keep your horse nice and warm at night by making sure he is rugged up according to the weather and whether he is clipped or not.

An icy yard can be dangerous – both for horses and their riders – so it's always a good idea to put extra grit on the ground.

Look out for layers of ice on the water trough. You'll need to break this on icy mornings so that your horse can have a drink!

In the winter, if your horse or pony lives out and is not clipped, always leave a certain amount of grease and dirt on his coat. This is natural protection, which will keep him warm and water-proofed.

Diet, good grooming, and staying warm will help your horse's coat stay glossy and shiny.

The best way to improve your technique is attention to detail. Listen carefully to your instructor's advice – even if it seems like something very small.

When jumping, try to work on balance and sitting in the middle of the saddle, rather than slightly to the left or to the right. Don't rely on your thighs and knees to grip with. Stay tall right up to the point of take-off.

Grid work is a great way to help improve your position over a fence. It can also really help your horse to improve the shape of his jump.

A bounce cross pole is an additional cross pole added immediately after a first, which means your horse will have to take off again straight after landing.

Whenever you ask your horse to jump a new type of fence, be sure to keep him in front of your leg (i.e. forward not fast) so he has time to assess the new jump. He will listen to your legs acting as an aid to tell him, 'Go on, everything is okay, trust me.'

Glossary

Mucking out (p.9) – Your horse or pony's stable needs mucking out once or twice a day, to remove droppings and wet bedding and then replace with fresh bedding.

Badminton Horse Trials (p.11) – A world class three day event comprising dressage, cross-country and show jumping, which takes place at the end of April or beginning of May each year in the park of Badminton House, Gloucestershire.

Burghley Horse Trials (p.11) – A world class three day event comprising dressage, cross-country and show jumping, which takes place in August or September each year in the park of Burghley House, Lincolnshire.

Flat racing (p.17) – Horse racing that does not involve steeplechase fences or hurdles, and there is no jumping involved.

Livery yard (p.24) – A stable that keeps horses, cares for and exercises them.

Grid work (p.31) – Small gymnastic jumping exercises which help to improve a horse's technique.

Trot poles (p.31) – Poles are placed on the ground and your horse has to lift his feet high enough to clear them. This really helps to improve a horse's rhythm in trot.

Grooming (p.40) – Regular grooming cleans your horse and will prevent him getting sore under tack. It keeps your horse healthy and comfortable and will help you form a relationship with him.

Body brush (p.40) – A soft brush for cleaning the grease and dust out of your horse or pony's coat. It can be used all over the body.

Mustang (p.48) – A free-roaming horse from the North-American West.

Head collar/halter (p.75) – This is used to lead a horse or pony, or tie it up, and usually made of leather or webbing.

Points of a Horse

1. poll
2. ear
3. eye
4. mane
5. crest
6. withers
7. back
8. loins
9. croup
10. dock
11. flank
12. tail
13. tendons
14. hock joint
15. stomach
16. elbow
17. heel
18. hoof
19. coronet band
20. pastern
21. fetlock joint
22. cannon bone
23. knee
24. shoulder
25. chin groove
26. nostril
27. muzzle
28. nose
29. cheekbone
30. forelock

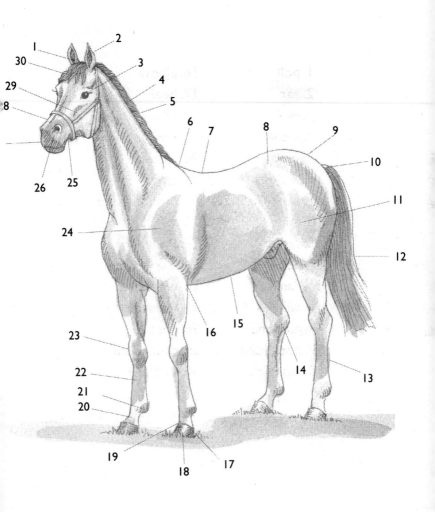

Pippa Funnell

"Winning is amazing for a minute, but then I am striving again to reach my next goal."

I began learning to ride when I was six, on a little pony called Pepsi.

When I was seven, I joined my local Pony Club – the perfect place to learn more about riding and caring for horses.

By the time I was fourteen and riding my first horse, Sir Barnaby, my dream of being an event rider was starting to take shape.

Two years later, I was offered the opportunity to train as a working pupil in Norfolk with Ruth McMullen, the legendary riding teacher. I jumped at the chance.

In 1987, Sir Barnaby and I won the individual gold together at the Young Rider European Championships, which was held in Poland.

Since then, hard work and determination have taken me all the way to the biggest eventing competitions in the world. I've been lucky and had success at major events like Bramham, Burghley, Badminton, Luhmühlen, Le Lion d'Angers, Hickstead, Blenheim, Windsor, Saumur, Pau, Kentucky – and the list goes on...

I married William Funnell in 1993. William is an international show jumper and horse breeder. He has helped me enormously with my show jumping. We live on a farm in the beautiful Surrey countryside – with lots of stables!

Every sportsman or woman's wildest dream is to be asked to represent their country at the Olympics. So in 2000, when I was chosen for the Sydney Olympics, I was delighted. It was even more special to be part of the silver medal winning team.

Then, in 2003, I became the first (and only) person to win eventing's most coveted prize – the Rolex Grand Slam. The Grand Slam (winning three of the big events in a row – Badminton, Kentucky and Burghley) is the only three-day eventing slam in the sporting world.

2004 saw another Olympics and another call-up. Team GB performed brilliantly again and won another well-deserved silver medal, and I was lucky enough to win an individual bronze.

Having had several years without any top horses, I spent my time producing youngsters, so it was great in 2010 when one of those came through – Redesigned, a handsome chestnut gelding. In June that year I won my third Bramham International Horse Trials title on Redesigned. We even managed a clear show jumping round in the pouring rain! By the end of 2010, Redesigned was on the squad for the World Championships in Kentucky where we finished fifth.

Today, as well as a hectic competition schedule, I'm also busy training horses for the future. At the Billy Stud, I work with my husband, William, and top breeder, Donal Barnwell, to produce top-class sport horses.

And in between all that I love writing the *Tilly's Pony Tails* books, and I'm also a trustee of World Horse Welfare, a fantastic charity dedicated to giving abused and neglected horses a second chance in life. For more information, visit their website at www.worldhorsewelfare.org.

Acknowledgements

Three years ago when my autobiography was
published I never imagined that I would find myself
writing children's books. Huge thanks go to Louisa
Leaman for helping me to bring Tilly to life, and
to Jennifer Miles for her wonderful illustrations.

Many thanks to Fiona Kennedy for persuading and
encouraging me to search my imagination and for all her
hard work, along with the rest of the team at Orion.
Due to my riding commitments I am not the easiest
person to get hold of as my agent Jonathan Marks
at MTC has found. It's a relief he has been able
to work on all the agreements for me.

Much of my thinking about Tilly has been done
out loud in front of family, friends and godchildren –
thank you all for listening.

More than anything I have to acknowledge my four-legged
friends – my horses. It is thanks to them, and the
great moments I have had with them, that I was able to
create a girl, Tilly, who like me follows her passions.

Pippa Funnell
Forest Green, February 2009

A SPECIAL MESSAGE FROM PIPPA

Hello PONY readers!

PONY is obviously Tilly's favourite magazine, and I hope you have enjoyed reading *Moonshadow*. You can find out about Tilly's other adventures at my website www.tillysponytails.co.uk. As well as lots of information about the books, you can catch-up with my latest news and find out where I'm competing.

You can also join the Tilly's Pony Tails club, and visit the Clubroom where there are some great activities, and you'll receive my newsletter.

I've been so busy with all my horses this year that I haven't had a lot of time for writing. But I'm delighted to be back with four brand new stories about Tilly and her beloved horse, Magic Spirit. The first book is called *Team Spirit*, and will be out in April 2014.

Happy riding and reading! See you soon

Coming soon . . .
a brand new Tilly adventure!

Tilly has had her beautiful grey, Magic Spirit, for over three years now and they're inseparable. She's thrilled they've been chosen for the Pony Club Eventing Championship team. Together with Ben, Kya and Anna, they face the challenges of dressage, cross country and show jumping against tough competition. And they learn that good teamwork is not always as easy as it looks.

OUT IN APRIL 2014

978 1 4440 1198 2

£4.99 paperback